# Bigfoot Sasquatch Files

## Volume 8

## By Kevin E. Lake

These stories are true.

Potentially...

changes made to any of these stories were in regard to the editing of typos, spelling and grammar, except in the cases where the author's local vernacular simply made for a better telling of the story than 'proper English' would have, thus, those parts were left alone.

Besides, only the Queen speaks proper English. But don't just take my word for it.

Ask her.

Enjoy!

1

## Why Now?

Two reasons.

Number one; I have enough of my own stories, and I always have had enough of my own stories, that I've never needed to tell the stories of others.

Number two; massive trust issues.

Look, I've worked in social media for more than a decade, and what I can tell you, is people are fake. Okay, that's true enough in real life, but when you allow people to hide behind a screen, up to thousands of miles away from your location, and you arm them with a  keyboard?

Man, you just upped the fake factor to infinity!

You have no idea who it is you're talking to on the other side of your computer screen. And I'm not talking about all the stuff they make reality television shows about- 'To Catch A Predator,' etc. I'm talking about on a much lower scale than that, even. But a scale where, if you derive the majority of your income from social media as a content creator, like I do, your time, which is your most valuable asset (though most humans don't realize this) is completely sucked out of you like the blood of a young damsel's neck in a b budget vampire flick.

Sadly, many of the folks who use social media, regularly, are merely bored. They're looking for unproductive ways to fill the great void of time that is their life, and what better way to do it than by scrolling, scrolling and then scrolling some more through stupid posts about cats on Fakebook (fingers crossed that *that* doomsday machine will be split up by the Government, and this author is a full supporter of capitalism- but Zuckerberg is an evil, pasty skinned little boy that needs to be stopped), or watching marginally creepy video after marginally creepy video on YouTube.

I'll tell you what better way.

By finding a content creator who posts those stupid memes about cats or who spends the majority of their working hours creating those marginally creepy videos who will engage them in communication. Yes, I'm talking about messaging or emailing back and forth.

Okay, this sounds cruel. And I know that there are people reading this right now who are my loyal, faithful subscribers on YouTube who watch every video I make and who've read every book I've ever written, etc. I'm not talking about you. I know, you're saying, 'how can you not be talking about me? I even leave comments regularly in the comment section of your videos.'

Look, that's what you call support. And I can tell by your comments that the overwhelming majority of you are healthy. You have a life. You come to my channel and you read my books for the very reason you should.

ENTERTAINMENT!

Now, with this said, does that mean that some of that sketchy stuff you've seen in some of our videos is fake?

Absolutely not!

What it means is healthy people know where to draw the line between understanding that content creators who share part of their lives with the masses (of strangers, at that) on social media are merely working in an industry that is still relatively new. They've (we've) harnessed the ability of technologies to basically support themselves (ourselves) by sharing part of themselves (ourselves), in a limited and harmless way.

But then there are the unhealthy people, and these people scare the hell out of me, and this is why we have never even considered accepting stories from other people, until now, and only by way of hand written or typed and printed and then mailed letters to our P.O. box, the address of which can be found in the description boxes of most of our videos on our YouTube channel.

You see, I've met some of the unhealthy people out there, and it's enough to make you look for another job!

I'll tell of this tale here, but never of YouTube. This is the tale of the first perhaps not so healthy individual we ever had experience with, in person, as YouTubers.

It was the summer of 2018. I'd recently gone viral with that whole 'neighbor with a crayon' video, and our channel was getting about ten thousand new subscribers a day! I had no idea what kind of videos to make at the time, because no one seemed to give a shit about our gardening videos or my wife's cooking videos (the trolls love to claim they do, telling us they liked our channel better when we made those types of videos, but numbers don't lie. Hm, let's see. My wife makes a cooking video and I make a gardening video, and both videos might get eight hundred views. We make a Bigfoot Sasquatch video and it gets eight thousand views. Where is our time better spent? And who's telling big fat bold face lies?- I might be 'crazy' but I'm not stupid).

Anyway, for some reason, it seemed people just liked hearing me talk, so I'd make videos where I would basically just tell stories of my life's experiences. The series was called "the morning ramble." It worked for a while, until I got sick and tired of the harassment from certain 'vertically challenged individuals who lived under bridges.' Many of them were actually dysfunctional blood relations and former friends and acquaintances from whom I've been estranged for many years who'd found me on YouTube by way of YouTube recommending they watch my videos. I guess they were like, "Hey, there's Kevin. Let's make fake profiles and go to his comment section and remind him of the absolute lowest points in his life, when he was really down and out, and of how much of a piece of shit he was back then, and let's let him know we've not forgotten, and that no matter how much he's cleaned his life up and turned things around and found happiness (and who knows, maybe even God?), that he's still just a worthless piece of shit, and he's not fooling anyone, no matter what this here YouTube's telling him!"

And that's exactly what they did.

Anyway, that's not even the scary part. That's the part to be expected by anyone who decides to bravely work in social media and put themselves out there. I mean, I've had people I knew and have not seen since college (a quarter of a century ago) try to reach out to me because of this gig.

Anyway, as you know, if you watch my videos, I have a tendency to digress and get off topic. So let me get back on at this time.

So, one day, while wrapping up my morning ramble, I mentioned that I needed to go, because my family and I were taking a trip. I actually said where we were going and when we'd be there. And when we got there?

Someone was waiting on us!

Seriously!

I won't say where this event took place, and if you've noticed that I don't disclose my locations on YouTube, it's not just because I'm trying to protect the location of any potential Bigfoot Sasquatches. I'm trying to protect myself and my family, and I learned to do so by way of this creeper, who we'll call Tom. That's not his real name, so that's the one we'll use.

So my family and I were at this place we'd gone to (it was a public event with hundreds of people in attendance), and we'd split up. After about ten minutes, I heard my wife say, "honey," and I looked over, and here comes my beautiful bride, Dearly, and our son, Daniel, and some old guy, about sixty, who looked like he was drugged up on all kinds of happy pills was walking with them. "We have a fan here," my wife said.

"Cool," I said, and what I was thinking was that someone who also happened to be attending the event for the day just happened to notice my family from our channel. This happens. Especially when we go into town in Charlottesville. We've had people come out of shops on the downtown mall and say hello, and tell us they watch our channel. We've run into people hiking in local trails who've told us the same. We run into people at the UVA football games who tell us they're our viewers. None of these people, not a single one of them, have ever creeped me out. They've always been kind, pleasant, and respectful of our space and our time. They basically say hello, tell us they watch, and then wish us a great day and continue on with theirs.

But not the *happy pill creeper* at the event I'm writing about here.

He'd gone to the event looking for us!

I know I have a tendency to make a short story long, as I've already done here, so I know it's too late to say long story short, but long story short, this guy happened to live not too far away from where the event we'd gone to was taking place. He told us he'd watched my morning ramble that morning and that when I'd said I was going to this event he decided he'd just hang out at the event all day until he ran into us.

Okay, that's not so creepy, right?

But then, he wouldn't leave us!

He followed us around the event like he was our best good buddy. He didn't just say hi and by and then leave. He literally never left, and he made us so uncomfortable, we decided to leave after we couldn't ditch the guy. We'd planned on staying all afternoon, but we split after about an hour of trying to ditch this guy.

But even then, he wouldn't stop!

He told us where he lived, and he told us that he wanted us to go home with him and meet his entire family. He explained that he had grandchildren our son's age, and that they should become best friends. At this point, he actually picked my son up, like he was his.

We were standing by the parking lot, and our car was in sight, and in my head, I knew that if this guy refused to put my son down, I was going to end up in jail, and I would be indicted for manslaughter.

I walked over and took my son from this creeper, and he actually relented, like he didn't want to let go. As if he was going to use Daniel as leverage to get us to go to his house and meet his family. I wrestled Daniel from his arms, and as we were making our way to our vehicle, this guy kept taking pictures of himself with us.

On the way home, Dearly and I decided there were certain precautions we needed to take if we were going to continue to be YouTubers. We decided we would NEVER say where we were going again. We decided that if we ever made videos while out and about in other cities, or while on vacation, that we wouldn't publish those videos until after we got home, not just so creepers wouldn't come looking for us, but also so no one would know we weren't home and try to rob our house in our absence.

If you knew how many people have contacted us and told us they know where we live, and they want to come meet us, or, more recently, even told us they know where they live and they love driving by and they get excited when they see us outside, but don't worry, they'll never stop, because, and this is their words, they're not crazy, it would absolutely blow your mind.

I've said recently that if I could support my family without having any social media presence, I wouldn't have any social media presence.

Anyway, I totally digress, but I hope this gives you more insight into why I rarely, if ever, engage viewers on our channel. I'd love to engage with the majority of you who are healthy, but the minority who are nut jobs scares the living shit out of me.

But, alas, and to my point!

I figured if anyone out there was willing to actually handwrite, or type, and then pay postage to send their story to a P.O. box, so that their story would actually get to me- in a very safe, non-stalkerish way- then, number one- they're not just bored, but sincere in wanting their story told, and, number two- there is probably some validity to it. Any vertically challenged individual who lives under a bridge can copy and paste some bullshit story about Bigfoot Sasquatch for shits and giggles, but it takes effort and time to go through the process of getting a story to me the way I've set it up for stories to get to me.

The good old fashioned way.

By way of an old fashioned letter.

By way of the old fashioned and outdated postal system (which I still hate, by the way, but I like many of the employees).

So, with no further do, as my beautiful bride Dearly, a.k.a. Giggly Girl would say, let's get to the stories!

2

## The Doctor's (retired) Story

*From a letter dated 12-02-2020.

Kevin,

It is my hope that I do not come across as if I'm talking down to you in this letter, either from the standpoint of a father figure, for I am old enough to be your father, or from the standpoint of my former profession before retirement. I worked for more than thirty years as a certified counsellor.

Further, I know you do not respond well to criticism. I am also tempering myself not to make this letter about diagnosing you. All I'll say in this regard is that I'd wager that you have a long, vast history of abusive, critical relationships that have left indelible scars on your psyche. Good news, my young friend. You are not alone. Many of us had fathers who were pricks. Bad news. Unless you get help with that some day, not only with the scars never leave, but the underlying wounds will never fully heal.

Well, so much for that effort.

However, before leaving this point, I do want to point out that some of the most creative individuals throughout history have been people who spend their childhoods being criticized by emotionally abusive parents, and by way of trying to prove to the world that they were worthy, and that they were okay at the endeavors they pursued, many of them changed the world. As a wise man once put it, "everyone can hear the music, but it is those who live outside of the box who create it." By the way, your book 'The Box' was my favorite book of yours. I'm surprised it's the one in your collection of many wonderful books you've written (and yes, I've read them all) that seems to have received the least amount of fanfare. However, I get it. Most folks who come to your literary works seem to do so by way of your YouTube endeavors, and I do know that that work centers almost entirely around the mythical creature which may or may not exist and which may or may not live in the woods behind your home.

Speaking of both your literary works and the 'creepy crawlies' on your land (and yes, that was an amazing video. It was the first of your videos I ever watched, and it was offered to me by way of YouTube recommendations), there was a story you wrote in one of your recent Bigfoot Sasquatch Files volumes that brought back memories from nearly three quarters of a century ago. The story I'm referencing was, I believe titled, "The Things We Leave Behind," or "Those We Leave Behind." Something to that effect. It was the story where you wrote of having to leave your best friend from childhood behind because you were both toxic for each other in regard to your addictions.

Firstly, if that story is true (and I have reason to believe the majority of what is put into most of your stories, even your novels, *is* true) I would like to point out as a former counsellor, and though I said in the opening of this communica that I would attempt to refrain from such things, you made the right decision. It was always so frustrating to me, when working with patients, when we would come so far in therapy, to the point where my patients were about to be 'healed' for the lack of a better term, because in this field there is no healing, rather, constant treatment, and then, the progress would stop, and usually emotional relapse would occur, because my patients simply refused to sever their ties with the most toxic people in their lives. Often, and most of the time, it was a toxic family member who was holding back my patient, and as difficult as it is to sever ties with spouses, parents and children (and I know you have first hand experiences with all of the above), it is of absolute necessity if one wants to truly get better, though as heartbreaking as it was to watch, the vast majority of the people I worked with throughout the years could not do this. I worked with people who I knew in my soul could have contributed to society in such a way that they would be remembered throughout the annals of history, yet they've spent their lives working in low wage, meaningless jobs, earning just enough to survive, because they've bought the lies that an abusive parent, spouse, or other family member sold them; they were worthless, their ideas were stupid, they were immature and irresponsible for wanting to pursue their passions, etc. And still others, who may not have gone on to achieve greatness, yet who could have known happiness, are, to this day, if they are still alive, miserable. And I don't even want to attempt counting up the number of funerals I have attended due to death at the hands of overdoses, accute alcoholism and suicide. I can only imagine that had you not cut ties with many of the people in your past, your funeral, had I known you personally, would have been another I would have attended.

However, I want to point out that it was not the character portrayed as the best friend of the main character in your story that brought memories rushing back from many years ago, rather, it was the quirky character of the honorary town cop in the story that brought back the memories. For you see, when I was a child, I knew a man just like that man, and the story of that man and things he claimed to see and know of are so strikingly similar to the real man that I knew, and his stories, that it's as if you were given a view into my very memories.

There is something else I must tell you about myself at this juncture, and the return address on the envelope in which this letter is enclosed may have given this away. I am Algonquin, and for centuries, my family has lived in the great lakes region, between the U.S. and Canada (and yes, I hate winters up here).

The man I knew, we simply called 'the old lunatic,' because that's what he was, and my family focussed on speaking English. Though I regret having lost some of our old ways, I do appreciate my parent's concern in my survival in modern times, and I was not able to simply survive, but I honestly feel as if I thrived throughout most of my life, yet this has nothing to do with the old lunatic, so I'll get back on track. It appears as if I may have been watching too many 'Crazy Lake' videos as of late with such a segway (just kidding… maybe).

So, for as early as I can remember, this was this man, the old lunatic, who was always digging holes in his yard. And I don't mean with a shovel. This guy had a backhoe. He would dig a hole about ten feet by ten feet by ten feet, and then he would bury it. At least this is what he appeared to be doing. When I once asked my father what the old lunatic was doing, he told me that the man was 'digging for dinosaur eggs.'

You might imagine that as a young child, I found this intriguing. Dinosaur eggs? What healthy, red blooded young boy wouldn't want a piece of that action? Around the time I turned twelve, my curiosity of the old lunatic and his endeavors had reached a boiling point, and one day, along with my childhood best friend, Steve, I approached the old lunatic and I engaged him in conversation.

What I discovered when talking to the old lunatic was that he was not a lunatic at all. He's what someone who lived life off of a reservation might refer to as a wealthy eccentric. He'd made a fortune off of a series of convenient stores back before convenient stores were even a regular thing, and though he did spend most of his time digging those giant holes in his yard and then covering them up, he was *not* digging for dinosaur eggs, it turned out, and he was *not* simply filling in those giant holes after he'd finished digging them for the sake of staying busy.

He was building traps.

And he was capturing and burying cryptids…

…alive!

Namely…

…wendigos!

The old man, whose name, by the way, was Robert, and who was no more a lunatic than you, Crazy Lake, are crazy, explained to us of how there were things in this world that most people will never believe in, mostly because they will never have any sort of experience with them. Robert went further and explained that there are so many people in the world who simply refuse to believe anything that they don't already believe, bigots he called them, and until then I thought that was a term referencing racists, but I learned that day, that a bigot is merely anyone who refuses to consider ways of thinking that are not already a part of the way they think- people who are unbending when it comes to different thoughts and the consideration of new or different ideas than their own. But Robert, that day, convinced Steve and me that he was a believer, and after hearing the story he told us, we were believers, too.

To make a long story short, unlike you in your videos (sorry, I had to put that in there), Robert's parents had been eaten by a wendigo. He told us these were creatures from our tribe's ancient legends. Basically, there is a form of bad energy that will consume a man, or a woman, who is already consumed with greed. It turns them into a monster; a flesh eating, cannibal, who must haunt the forests and eat human beings, and despite how much they eat, they are never satiated. Just like people who suffer from the deadly sin of greed are never satisfied with having enough, no matter how much stuff they acquire, the wendigo is never full, no matter how much they eat.

That day, Steve and I picked up shovels and began helping Robert dig and set his traps. In time, he would teach us to operate his backhoe.

But then something happened.

Steve and I got older. We stopped believing. And when we did, we realized that Robert was not an old sage. Robert, we would now agree with the rest of our community, was an old lunatic.

We were not rude to Robert, like the two boys were in the story you wrote about the kids who had a similar relationship with the honorary town cop who everyone thought was crazy. And just as it turned out that your town cop wasn't crazy, but right in what he saw and experienced (sorry for the spoiler alert for anyone who hasn't read Bigfoot Sasquatch Files Volume 6 yet), Robert had been correct and honest about what he'd seen and experienced as well.

I remember receiving a call from Steve, years later, when I was in graduate school at the University of Wisconsin, working on my masters degree in psychology. He called to tell me not just that Robert, the old lunatic, had died, because as it turned out, Robert had died more than two years before that- I simply had never heard of his passing- but of what they found in Robert's back yard.

It turns out that they were clearing the land to build a subdivision type of neighborhood. And just like Robert's convenient store chain, this was back in a time when subdivisions were not even a thing yet. And when they began digging to lay the foundations and build the basements of the new houses that were going to be built in the area, according to Steve, they found skeletons...

...everywhere!

So if you've read my letter this far, I know what you might be thinking. Robert was a serial killer, and Steve and I had been accomplices, albeit unknowingly, in hiding some of his victims' bodies. This was not the case. For you see? As Steve explained to me, they could not identify the skeletons. Sure, they were human-like, but they were not human. And many of them had- and make sure you are sitting down for this part- deer like antlers attached to their skulls. However, they'd not been artificially attached, as if some sort of sadistic ritual had taken place before their murders.

They were bonafide parts of the skulls!

They'd grown there!

You can Google my story all you want, Kevin, and you will not find evidence of it on the internet. This all happened long before you were born, and since it happened in one of our sovereign communities, this story would have never leaked to the press. You see, that's one thing about my people that hasn't changed. We do not air our dirty laundry.

Kevin, I know your channel focuses on Bigfoot Sasquatch. I know that you think you may or may not have a Bigfoot Sasquatch or a clan of Bigfoot Sasquatches living in the woods behind your house. And to be honest with you, I don't even know if you honestly believe this or not, or if you're putting us all on. And I'm not trying to be one of those "vertically challenged individuals who live under bridges" as you refer to the degenerates who troll your channel. I'm just being honest, and I hope you can appreciate that.

However, I do know that there have been times in your videos when I could tell that you were genuinely, and flat out, as you southerners like to say, scared. And I know it was genuine. Remember, I was a counsellor. And what I'll say, going out on a limb here, is that though one can fake monsters in the woods, and though one can genuinely act scared, one cannot really be scared unless they are truly scared, and I have seen that in you in many of your videos.

Also, I have seen things in your videos. And I have heard the screams of the 'mysterious creatures in the woods,' as you refer to them, and these things I've seen and heard in your videos bring back memories from my childhood. Things I'd hear late at night in the great lakes region- the home of my youth- and things I'd catch a mere glimpse of out of the corner of my eyes in the same place.

Kevin, please be careful. Again, I do not think you are crazy in any way. Frankly, I consider your work a sign of genius. However, I do believe it is crazy to continue to go into those woods alone, all for the sake of making your videos that I feel not enough people truly appreciate, not knowing exactly what it may or may not be, as you would say, that you are dealing with. For you see, I do believe I know what you are dealing with, and it is not, in my humble opinion, a Bigfoot Sasquatch. It is, rather…

…the wendigo.

Sincerely yours,

Peter S. (last name omitted)

The End

3

Homesick

*From a letter dated: December 2, 2020

Dear Kevin,

I can't remember when or why I started watching your channel. I know I've been a regular viewer for about three years now. So I must have started watching before all of this "Bigfoot Sasquatch" stuff, as you call it, started.

I remember why I kept watching, though. Your videos made me homesick!

I have lived my whole life in Morgantown, West Virginia. I know our states border each other, but it's quite a drive from where I live down to your neck of the woods. I know this well, because my parents were both from the south western part of Virginia. A town named Christiansburg, which is not too far from Blacksburg. Home of those dreaded Virginia Tech Hokies. As you might imagine, being a West Virginia Mountaineer, I hate the Hokies as much if not more than you probably do, since you live in Charlottesville, or thereabouts. However, don't think for a minute that I'm any fan of the UVA Cavaliers, because I'm not.

Okay, sports talk aside (and honestly, I don't really care about any of it, but I know you like your UVA hats), watching your videos, especially the ones that have you and your wife and your son in them, on your homestead, brings back so many memories from the summers I would spend with my grandparents down in Christiansburg. The videos you guys have made of fishing on the local rivers in your area reminds me of all the times my grandfather would drive us over to the New River, on the southern border of West Virginia to go fishing. Those years, some fifty years past now, were a magical time in my life.

I'll admit that once you started this "Bigfoot Sasquatch" stuff, originally, I unsubscribed from your channel. I'm sorry to say, but I also left a comment on the last video I watched telling you that I was unsubscribing. I know that you banned me, because when I returned to your channel only a few months later (it was winter, and I was up to my ass in snow, and I couldn't stay away from the views of those much milder winters in Virginia that I could see daily on your channel) I tried to comment and I could not. I don't blame you for banning me. I was negative. I could have unsubscribed and moved on, but I felt that I had to get a dig in at you. It was immature, and I'm sorry. I can't imagine how many 'vertically challenged individuals who live under bridges' you have to deal with, and it wasn't right for me to have been one of them. If you ever feel like unbanning me (my YouTube userid is FatJack55) I promise, I won't do it again.

Now, with sports talk and past grievances aside, it's time for me to get to my point. Like you, I've always had an issue with that, but alas, we're two salty old souls adrift in this great vast universe who were meant to be connected. Potentially. (hehehe)

I had completely forgotten about all the stories that my grandfather used to tell my sister and me when we'd go camping at night, either on our grandparent's farm or on the banks of the New River. It was only during this past Thanksgiving, when I was talking to my sister on the phone (goddamn Covid) that I was reminded, because she reminded me.

Sadly, once I'd reached my teens, I no longer wanted to go to my grandparents' place down in Christiansburg for the summers. I had friends. I had a girlfriend (who, by the way, is now my wife), and I was playing sports. The last thing I wanted to do was hang out with an old couple who had funny accents (listen to me, a 'dumb hillbilly' as I know you know we're known outside of West Virginia calling the kettle black), who sat on their porch talking about how danged hot it was most of the summer and listening to what I thought was a half crazy old man telling stories about things that do not exist most evenings.

The summer of my senior year of high school, my sister, two years younger than me, went and spent the summer, alone, with my grandparents. Our parents had recently gotten divorced (a rare occurrence in my youth, but an event my generation, the baby boomers, would make quite popular) and I guilt shamed my mother into allowing me to stay in Morgantown. She worked almost all the time, so I got to spend all my time with my girlfriend. We ended up "getting in trouble" if you know what I mean, and it sped up the "I do's" at the altar, but I don't regret any of it. And I'm proud to say that she and I are still together, having never participated in the divorce game, and we have three kids, all of which are about your age.

My little sister came back with quite the tale at the end of that summer. Allegedly, she and our grandfather, while out camping early in the summer, were visited by someone or something that would walk circles around their tent at night. At first, they thought it was a deer or a bear passing through. However, the first night it happened, it happened for the entire night. Whatever was walking around the tent did not leave until just before dawn.

Our grandfather had fallen asleep, convinced that what they were hearing was merely an animal, but my sister, she told me, was too scared to sleep. I know Morgantown is not a big city as far as big cities go, but we did live in the middle of town, and we didn't have deer walking around in our yard at night.

A week later, my sister and grandfather went camping again. They were camping on our grandparent's property, so the likelihood of what they'd heard being a trespasser was small. You know, living in Virginia yourself, that people there do not trespass, because they know they are more likely to get shot for so doing than not, and that was even more true back in those days.

Anyway, my sister and grandfather tried an experiment. They left a half dozen apples out, about twenty yards from their tent, as well as a candy bar. Yes, a candy bar.

My little sister thought the idea of leaving a candy bar out was as crazy as you probably do reading this, but my grandfather's point was that any animal could eat the apples without leaving any sort of trace of what, specifically, at the apples, but if anything ate the candy bar, you would clearly be able to tell it was an animal by the way it would have to maul the wrapper to get to the food inside. Most animals, my grandfather said, wouldn't even touch a candy bar.

The next morning, my sister and grandfather found no apples and only the wrapper from the candy bar. And it had not been mauled and gnawed on, as if from an animal, like a bear or a racoon. It had been opened, neatly, by someone or something which obviously had opposable thumbs!

When my sister and grandfather told me of this tale when I went down to Christiansburg with my mother to pick my sister up at the end of that summer, I thought it was all just a bunch of bull they'd made up in order to make me feel guilty for not having gone down and spent the summer on my grandparent's farm. I did not believe it for a minute, and I let them know about it. They didn't seem to care that I didn't believe. They said it would always be something special between the two of them. When they made not a single effort to try to convince me to believe, I thought there might actually be some truth to it.

I would go on to college after high school (Go Mountaineers!), and my grandfather passed away during my senior year. My grandmother passed away only six months later. We believe she died of a broken heart, as she and my grandfather had been together since childhood.

I attended my grandfather's funeral. It was actually held at his farm. He'd wanted to be buried at the top of a hill overlooking the old farmhouse. Ironically, it was one of the locations where we'd often camp when I spent the summers there, and it was the same location where he and my little sister had claimed to have had their experience with what I'd jokingly call the 'candy bar eating Bigfoot,' which I'm sure you'd call the 'candy bar eating Bigfoot Sasquatch.'

There were not a whole lot of people in attendance for my grandfather's funeral. He was a shy, private man. He didn't have many friends, but the ones he had were close. Ironically, I think that's another reason I found myself drawn to your YouTube channel. You kind of remind me of him.

After the funeral, a few people walked over and put flowers beside the headstone of my grandfather's grave. My little sister placed a candy bar on top of it. Though the jury of my mind was still out on the validity of their story from years before, I found her gesture sweet and sincere, and it brought tears to my eyes.

That evening, my little sister and I sat on the old porch swing on the front porch of the old farmhouse. We talked well into the night, mostly reminiscing about all the summer's we'd spent on the farm. We went to bed just before midnight.

Some time in the middle of the night, I was awakened by what sounded like a loud stomp on the front porch. The room my sister and I were sleeping in was the master bedroom of the house, which was on the first floor. The window looked out over the porch.

After hearing the stomp, I raised my head to look out the window, but it was pitch black dark outside. There was no moon. I could see nothing. I lay my head back on my pillow and went back to sleep as quickly as I had awakened.

The next morning, I rose early. I wanted to take advantage of seeing the sunrise over my grandparent's farm, so I made my way out to the front porch and I sat in the old porch swing. When I rested my hands beside me on the swing, I felt something with the fingertips of my left hand. I instinctively wrapped my fingers around what was there, and I raised it to my face.

It was a candy bar wrapper!

To this day, I have no idea how the candy bar wrapper got on the swing. I never asked my sister about it, for you see, part of me believed the story she and our grandfather had told me. I erred to the side of caution, and I viewed the wrapper as having been left as a message for my sister, so I left it on the swing.

I watched, shortly after my sister woke that morning, as she, too, made her way to the porch swing. I peered through the bedroom window, making sure to do so from the opposite side of the room as the window so that my sister would not see me, and I saw that she took up the wrapper, and when she did, she cried.

At long last, I had my answer, as far as whether or not their story had been true.

I also believe that I've had confirmation about their story being true. Did I see the Bigfoot Sasquatch myself?

No!

Then what's the confirmation?

My sister never mentioned the wrapper that she found on the porch swing to me, and to this day, I've never asked her about it. As they say, some things are better left unsaid, and in this case, I believe that what is being left unsaid is the truth.

Kevin, thank you so much for the time you put into making your videos. The memories some of them have brought back to me are worth a priceless fortune. I would imagine there are better things you could be doing with your time, but I, for one, appreciate every minute that you put into your videos.

Though you've banned me, I'll be a viewer for life!

Kindest Regards

J.S.

Morgantown, WV

Faces In The Fields And Forest

*Author's explanation: I have always felt that there are things, if not beings, for a better word, around us, that cannot necessarily be seen, heard, or even understood. This is a touchy subject, because so many people who believe in just about anything think that their way is the only way, and the minute you mention anything about other realms, dimensions, planets with life, the spirit world, or cryptids, you are written off, not just as crazy, but as demonic, a satanist, an occultist, a true lunatic whose soul (if these exist) is hellbound (if that place exists).

I'm going to go out on a limb here, but could it be possible, just, well, I'll say potentially, because I love that word so much, that all that Bible stuff is true, as is all the other stuff that cannot be explained? I'm not trying to offend anyone who believes in Jesus and all that stuff, as I do myself, but just because one states a belief in one idea or concept, it does not believe that one does not believe in another. In a word, it's okay to believe in multiple explanations, especially when it comes to things that cannot necessarily be explained (I know that sounds like an oxymoron, but I know what I'm doing here), without having to state your abandonment in other beliefs. Remember, the more we learn, the more we realize we don't know, and I know most people's absolute, bullheaded, stubborn refusal to believe in concepts they don't already know, understand or believe in (the word is bigotry) is based in the fear of realizing just how much is out there that they don't know about or understand.

"If it ain't mentioned in the Bible, then it ain't real." That's a quote. Who said it? Damn near every adult in my circle of influence while growing up in Appalachiastan. Not trying to knock them, but geez, there's a reason I left, and the last time I read my Bible (yes, I actually have), I saw no mention of the internet, social media, electricity or cancer.

Just sayin'.

For a long time I've simply felt that some have the eyes to see and the ears to hear, while so many do not. And I'm talking in the literal sense here, not just the anti-bigot sense. Some people can literally see things that are there, that remain hidden to others, and hear some of these things as well.

One such phenomena that fits into this description would be faces in the fields and forests surrounding my homestead. And I'm sure there are plenty of these faces everywhere else around the world. I know I've seen them in the Middle East and Southeast Asia.

One thing I've gotten in the habit of doing is making sure not to look any of these faces in the eye. Well, the ones that have eyes, because some of them don't, and those are the ones that can be a bit terrifying.

Now, am I alone in seeing these faces?

Absolutely not!

For years, we have been having viewers of our YouTube channel, Homesteading Off The Grid, comment in the comment section that they, too, have seen faces in our fields and forests. And these comments were coming in long before we ever got on the Bigfoot Sasquatch kick. I'm talking about back when we made all those exciting videos about corn and green beans! (uh-hem).

Recently, one of our viewers, a lady by the name of Brittany, contacted us and sent us pictures of some of the actual faces in our field and forest that she was able to isolate on film, somehow, from our videos. If you would like to see these faces, if you've not already, simply go to our YouTube channel and watch a video called "Disturbing Images Submitted By Obserant Viewer Is Proof That Things Are Worse Than Imagined." Not to mention, if you watch that video, you'll hear about one hell of a crazy dream I remember having had at the age of four, forty three years ago, as of this writing.

Here, printed with permission, is some of the communication I received from Brittany:

"Hi Kevin,

My name is Brittany. It's a pleasure to meet you. I've enjoyed your channel since the very beginning with the bunnies and Roger. I was working with behaviorally challenged bunnies, cats, dogs, lizards, chinchillas, rats, etc. I am furloughed from my job due to Covid.

Some people consider me to be empathic or clairvoyant. I just think I'm Brittany. I can pick up on weird things quickly, like you, and from the start saw things like you did. I spent too many years hiding the true "me" and ignored my gut instincts because I didn't want to be seen as a weirdo. My boss from my Animal Shelter dog—who is a Shaman/Holistic Healer and a real paranormal investigator encouraged me to use my "gifts" which I didn't know I had. Now that I've seen how the world really works and operates I sometimes miss the days of being blissfully ignorant. c'est la vie!

How do you stay sober with all the creepy going on around you? Some of those faces are terrifying, like the yellow eyed wendigo /werewolf thingy.

Speaking of faces. You have one dude that follows you constantly. I think he's the one playing the pranks and throwing walnuts. I also believe he is the ringleader of the bunch. Wherever he goes, the Yeti army goes. I think the dude is alien. Ya know your video that shows a strange creature standing next to the life size Halloween figures in your yard.....well... that's him.

I will enclose some alien races he could be a part of. I call him Kermit, because he looks like Kermit the frog. Wherever he goes, the army of Squatch is sure to follow...

I have just been filtering screenshots.

I see the moving blurs, faint faces, and lots of eyeballs. I was genuinely frightened by some things I uncovered. Your scariest video is the one where Kermit jumped into the tree and left that freaky carving of himself (he looks like that too!) I could see frustration and fear in your face. I deal with a similar but different situation. Nothing is more stressful than someone or something insinuating itself into your life, and the life of your loved ones. What's worse is when that unseen force is causing a multitude of problems, and the people around don't believe you because you don't have clear cut photographic evidence. Your wife seems like a doll...and your son is adorable. It's hard to see you guys dealing with that (and then trolls running their mouths). I just want you to know, it's not you. That stuff is there and it's scary. Plus you're a dad and a husband, and your first priority is keeping them safe and sound.

Like you said in your uploads, the craziness becomes a part of your life. It starts to blend into the background like white noise. I love that you use humour as a way to offset the absurdity of the situation. Dearly is a great support. It's great to see that.

I don't know if my images will be of help. I'm not a crazy fan girl type. I hate the spotlight and I've had my share of stalkers.

*(This portion of Brittany's message is being withheld, as she mentions some of the specifics about the stalkers I shared with her we've dealt with in the past, and two of them are involved in pending legal actions, so we cannot disclose details here).*

I'll send you a couple pics. If I attach them to the letter—I'll somehow erase all the texts.

Thank you, and I hope you and your family have a wonderful morning.

Brittany

***

*Author's note (again): Brittany, by far, is NOT the only viewer who has spotted faces in our fields and forest. Below is a list of other comments that have been left on our channel in this regard. These comments have been left over the years on many, many different videos.

~ I have been watching your channel, with interest, for about four months now. I have never seen the Bigfoot Sasquatch you claim may or may not live in the woods behind your home, so I'm leaning toward the 'may not' part of that statement. However, I cannot help but notice that you have many, many faces in the forest behind your home. They are even in the trees. I believe they are demonic in nature, so please be careful.

~ I am a believer in all things Bigfoot Sasquatch, but I don't believe this guy. I think he's nuttier than a squirrel turd. But I see lots of faces in his field. Freaky. I thought he was doing some kind of editing at first, but there's no way these things can be edited into the video like this. Some of them are scary. I know I see them. But fuck this guy. He's crazy.

~ I know Bigfoot is real. Down here in Louisiana where I live we have something similar. It's called the skunk ape. I've never seen the skunk ape, but I know it's real, because he raped my cousin. I don't believe a word this crazy legs says in these videos, and I think he's making fun of those of us who believe, but I see a lot of weird things in the background behind him. Like faces.

~ I hope that one of these days this ass clown comes face to face with a real bigfoot and it tears him limb to limb. But can anyone else see all those faces? Why doesn't he talk about those? Bigfoot is real, but there's not one in this guy's yard, but there sure are a lot of faces.

~ Kevin I love your videos. I watch every one of them. I don't care if they are about gardening or Bigfoot or fishing. I love them all. I have to admit, I'm not buying into the Bigfoot stuff, but I'll also admit that I have seen a few things in your videos that are kind of creepy. Also, there have been times when I could tell you were seriously scared. In one of your videos, you kept looking behind you saying you were being followed. I didn't see Bigfoot, because Bigfoot isn't real, and I have reason to believe you know that, but it looked like there was this really creepy mist following you. When you would stop, the mist would disappear. And then when you started walking again, it would reappear, and then form into a face, and then form back into mist and follow you again. I don't know if that's something you're doing with editing or what, but it's kind of creepy. Be careful.

~ Your wife's laugh is infectious. I can understand why she doesn't like to go into the woods and do a lot of videos with you anymore. I see the faces in the trees. Please don't point them out to her. I'm afraid she would get so scared if she saw them she would go running back to Puerto Rico.

*Author's note- my wife is from the Philippines.

~ This guy is a fake and a fraud and he is going to lose everything once he's properly exposed. But what the fuck is up with all those faces in his woods?

~ Kevin, I wish you would stop doing those night hunts. Every time you point out that the temperature drops, and a mist moves in, I can see faces in the mist. I don't believe in Bigfoot, and I don't think that you really do either. I know that it gets you views on YouTube and that translates to money and you need that to take care of your family. However, I don't think it's worth the continued risks you take, especially at night, to make these videos. The faces that surround you in the mist at night appear to be dominic in nature, and I fear they are set upon dring you even crazier than you already claim to be, which, I don't believe you are either.

~ First and foremost, this guy is fake and so is his videos. How stupid does he think we are? Bigfoot? Seriously? The next thing you know, he is going to be making videos claiming that the Loch Ness Monster lives in that little pud puddle of a pond in front of his house. But what the fuck is up with all the faces I see hovering just above the ground all over his fields?

~Don't you people get it? Bigfoot is real, but it's assholes like this guy that make it so hard to believe those of us who have actually encountered the real thing. This asshat is nothing more than some douchebag crying wolf. The best thing we could do to stop him is band together and stop watching his videos. He gets paid for this. By watching his videos, we are encouraging bad behavior. I for one will never, ever, EVER watch another one of this asshole's videos again. But what the fuck is up with all the faces in his fields and forest?

*Author's note (again, times two): The list could go on indefinitely, but I'll stop because I'm sure you now get the point. I'm suck. I'm fucking crazy, because at times, I think I may see what may or may not be Bigfoot in the forest and fields behind my home. And that, obviously, makes me certifiable. But, by God, there are goddamn faces everywhere!

The End

# The Crazy Bird Lady

*From a letter dated January 4, 2021

Hi Kevin,

Give my regards to your giggly wife and your adorable son. It's easy to see why a man as blessed as you are, having those two special people in your life, is always so happy, despite the level of crap you have to put up with from assholes who are miserable and who obviously hate their lives, on YouTube.

As I sit and write you this letter (thank you for finally getting a P.O. Box, because I'm a little older, and I still like letters, and I don't trust that there internet) I am sitting in my screened in and heated front porch, watching birds and squirrels at the various bird feeders in my front yard. Like you, I have assholes for neighbors, so I had a fence put up years ago so I didn't have to see the bastards. I found that just the sight of them made me angry. So I blocked the sight of the sonsabitches. But the fence looked very impersonal, so I planted a few bushes in front of it and then hung bird feeders, and little did I know, over the course of the last ten years or so since I did all this, I would become an avid bird watcher. The only problem? Those asshole neighbors had an asshole cat that used to come around the fence and eat my birds.

One of my granddaughters happened to be over one weekend about a year or so ago, completely ignoring me while she stayed glued to her smartphone. I asked her what she was watching that was so important it would draw her into ignoring her dear old grandmother, and she said YouTube. I asked her what was on that, and she said everything. I asked her if there was a way to keep asshole neighbors' asshole cats from eating your birds at your feeder and she typed a few buttons and then gave me her phone. She had pulled up a video of you showing how you piled sticks around your feeders to keep your asshole cat from eating your birds.

And if you haven't been able to tell, though people write me off as the crazy cat lady of my neighborhood, because I don't go out much, and I get a lot of mail, I'm anything but. I absolutely hate cats. Their assholes!

My granddaughter said she needed some fresh air, so she went out in the backyard. I know that what she really meant was that she needed to go smoke some of that Mary Jane. So when she didn't come back quickly, and your video went off, your next video came up. I think it was how to keep your windows from fogging up in cold weather, or something. But I kept watching, because my granddaughter was still out back toking up, as I've heard her call it. And then when the next video came on, and it was yours, it was something about Bigfoot Sasquatch.

I remember at first asking myself how someone could be so smart and yet so stupid at the same time. I mean, Bigfoot Sasquatch? Are you for real?

When my granddaughter came back in, high as a kite, I gave the phone back to her and I told her what I thought of you. Both smart but dumb, and she asked me if I wanted her to troll you. I asked her what that meant, and she said she would call you a cocksucker in the comment section, but I told her there was no need to be rude. You seemed like an okay guy, just a bit off your rocker. But aren't we all sometimes?

Well, just a month later was Christmas, and that spoiled ass daughter of mine bought that spoiled ass daughter of hers, the chain toker, a new smartphone even though there was nothing wrong with her old one, so the little chain toker, and her name's Serena, by the way, gave me her old phone. I told her to teach me how to use that YouTube thing so I could see if you'd either been committed or solved the problem of world poverty yet, and I'll be a son of a saint if I didn't find that I quite enjoyed your videos more than I could have ever imagined. A lot of it might be that I didn't know how to use the phone or the YouTube too good and I was afraid to touch anything, and your videos just kept playing, one after the other. I'll go on and admit it. I'm as hooked to your videos as my granddaughter is the Mary Jane.

Now, back to my birdfeeders.

At first, I thought it was just my imagination playing tricks on me. Maybe my mind was being influenced by all your silly videos. Or maybe I had inhaled some of Serena's second hand smoke. But I swear to the Arc Angel Michael that just before dark, about a week ago, I looked up and I saw something large, dark and seemingly ominous out there at my bird feeders. My sighting only lasted a second. It looked like I caught the him, her or it (it wasn't a they, because there was just one of them) holding up one of my danged bird feeders, shaking the seeds out of it and into their mouth, just like you or I might do with a potato chip bag once we'd eaten all the chips and want to suck down the crumbs.

Then, just like that, it was gone!

Now, reason kicked in pretty quick, and I told myself there's no such thing as a Bigfoot, or a Sasquatch, and there definitely ain't no such thing as a Bigfoot Sasquatch, like you're always a'callin' it. So I knew it had to be my asshole neighbor. Much like you've described one of your asshole neighbors, I refer to this man as the smartest guy in the room. He knows everything about everything, even though he's done nothing and does nothing. I reckon he has a lot of dignity, and he prefers to sit around on it all day long. He's got him one of them women that likes wearing the pants in the family taking care of him. I guess it's win win. He gets to do nothing, and she gets to brag about how she's superior and all that. Hell, my husband, before he passed, never minded digging a ditch if that's what he needed to do to take care of his family, and I was damn proud of him for doing it.

I figured I'd confront that asshole. I should have years ago. Could have saved me money on that fence, though I do enjoy watching the birds.

Anyway, I go over there, and I'll be damned if not just the neighbors aren't there anymore, but the house isn't there anymore, either!

While I was standing there, wondering how a whole damn house could vanish without me noticing, though as I've already told you, I don't go out much and I get a lot of mail, I noticed that another neighbor further down, a woman, was looking at me, so I waved to her. She came over and asked if I was okay. I guess maybe she thought I wasn't because I was standing out in the cold with my bathrobe on over my nightgown and I was in my favorite pair of pink bunny house slippers. Leaning on my walker and all. Looking all crazy myself, I guess, 'cause my hair was a mess.

I told that lady that came over to check on me that I was just fine and not to touch me, but I asked what happened to the house that used to be there, too, and she said it burned down. Now, how in the hell can the house right beside me burn down and me not know about it, is what I asked her. She looked embarrassed for me (I know the look), and she said that sometimes people just miss things.

"Well did you miss the Bigfoot Sasquatch that just came a runnin' around the side of my fence?" I asked her. She looked at me, her jaw lookin' like it might fall off entirely, the way she was a holdin' her mouth open, and I said, "Well, did ya?"

"I saw something," she said, and then she just kept looking at me like I was senile, which, hell, I guess I might be, but at least she shut her damn mouth. She was starting to look like someone who'd been touched. I don't know if you can say that these days, but back in my time, that's exactly what we would have called her. Touched.

Well, the woman's husband came over just as I was turning around to go back around my side of the fence. He was yelling something about seeing something. I just turned around and looked at him and told him if he had something to say then just say it, and that's when he told me that him and a couple of the other neighbors had been seeing whatever I thought I'd seen.

"It comes around in the winter," the man said. "It seems to like bird seed."

"You're kidding me," I said.

"I know, right?" the man said. Now just what in the hell does that even mean? I know right?

By the way, I asked him how the house on the other side of my fence had burned. He told me the smartest guy in the room had set it on fire. He tried to make it look like an accident so he could collect insurance money, because I guess that miss 'bring home the bacon and fry it up in a pan bitch' he'd married had given him an ultimatum. Either contribute to the household, financially, or find some other woman who would take him in based upon his all knowing intellect. I guess he's doing time somewhere. And, according to my other neighbors, his wife done went and shacked up with some woman she works with. Oh well. As the world turns.

Anyway. I just wanted to let you know that I love your YouTube channel, and not just because it's the only one I know how to watch. You're okay to look at. Pretty easy on the eyes. Not that I'd expect you to know what that even means, but you can always go ask an old lady.

Take Care,

J.P.

Barboursville, West "By God" Virginia (or as you'd say,
Appalachiastan)


The End


6


John's Story

*From a letter dated January 5, 2021


Dear Kevin,

I hope this letter reaches you. As you can tell, I do not want you to
know my location, or any true specifics about me. I'll refer to myself
as John, because that is not my real name.

I absolutely have to tell you my story. You have no idea how happy I
am that you set up a post office box so I could mail you this letter.
Though I've been watching your YouTube channel for three years
now, I have never commented and I have never subscribed. I will
never do either on your channel or anyone else's. I do not leave
tracks on the internet, because they know everything about
everybody when you do that. I don't even have a sign in for
YouTube. I simply search out your channel and videos from the
search box.

Okay, so here's the deal.

The Bigfoots and aliens and faces on your property and all the other weird things you see are holograms. I know how they look, because they are showing them to me, too.

I know that you were in the military, and I know that you were in other parts of the world doing some really badass shit, and I thank you for your service, but I know that you have also seen things that you are probably not supposed to talk about. And the thing is, they are afraid you are going to talk about them, so they want to discredit you. They want to make you look crazy so that if you talk about some of the stuff you saw or that you may have done overseas, everyone will think you're lying, because you believe you have a Bigfoot Sasquatch, among other things, in your backyard.

I know this, because they're doing it to me, too!

Now, I'll admit, I never served in the armed forces, though I very much wanted to. My father was a Naval officer, and I was in ROTC in high school and college, but I never actually served after that. You see? I was too smart, and I don't follow orders well, and they knew it, based on various aptitude tests I was given while I was in ROTC in college.

Basically, and to keep it simple, they viewed me as a dangerous threat. My IQ is higher than anyone else you've ever met. And aside from simply being highly intelligent, I also know how to think for myself, and I do so on a regular basis.

This would make for a very poor fit with the military. If they told me what to do, and I knew it was not the right thing to do, then I wouldn't do it. It's just that simple. And then the military industrial complex would not be able to achieve their total goal of world domination. I would be the burr under their saddle. The chink in their armor. And they knew all this, so they did the exact same thing to me that they've been doing to you.

I never leave my house, unless I run out of beer, because every time I go out I see images of their destruction. With you, they show you Bigfoot and aliens. With me? They show holograms of my yard being ocean front property, and I live at least a thousand miles in from the coast. I believe they do this, because they track me on the internet, using my IP address, and they know that global warming is of great concern to me. They fear that if I sound the alarm about how serious this problem really is, the masses might listen to me, because they would be able to tell how smart I am just from listening to me talk, so they project these holograms from outer space, with a satellite they keep hovering over my house, so they can discredit me if I were to sound the alarm.

Let me tell you, Kevin, these people are dangerous. I can only imagine some of the things you may have done or seen while you were in the military. Things they absolutely do not want the general public to know. I'm convinced that if they were to view you as enough of a threat, they would kill you. Please don't let it come to that.

I know you probably think I'm crazy, but I'm not. This is a deep state military operation called MK-Ultra, and my friend, you have been part of it for a long time, you are probably just now finding out about it.

Google it. You'll see.

Take care, and please keep making your videos. Though I know Bigfoot is not real, and you're only seeing holograms, I do find your videos entertaining. They help me pass the time while I stay secluded in my humble home, mostly in the basement.

John.

The End

## 7

I Know He's Real But You Don't Got One


*From a letter dated January 5, 2021


Kevin,

You have summarily banned six of my various fake profiles, but I know you'll read this letter. You cannot get rid of me as easily as the stroke of a mouse click.

I know Bigfoot is real. And that's what it's called. Bigfoot. Not Bigfoot Sasquatch, you buffoon!

And I know he's real, because I've seen him!

I was a logger back in Maine when I saw him. I had been on the job for a year. I was out in the woods, by myself, because my team had gone into town for lunch. We were logging a stand of timber not too far away from a small community that had a Subway, so they wanted to get sandwiches.

I remember laying my back up against my backpack. I don't remember falling to sleep. But I do remember waking up, and seeing that eight feet tall, probably eight hundred pound monstrosity standing over me, looking down at me as if he was wondering what I was doing trespassing.

The only thing that saved me was that my buddies were coming back at that very instant and when the thing standing over me heard the truck, it took off running into the forest.

Now, here's the part about you that really pisses me off, and it's why you'll never stop hearing from me. I was a good worker. The best. And I had big plans. I wanted to become a foreman and then a manager after that. I aspired to gain all the knowledge about timbering that I could and then eventually start my own logging company. But no. None of that was to be. For you see? When I told my friends about what I had seen, lumbering over me, pun intended as your dumbass might say, I became the laughing stock not just of our small timbering operation, but of our small town back home, about two hours south of where we were working that day.

My sighting occurred more than a decade ago, and to this day, because of it, I am still merely a worker bee. My income has barely increased since the time I started on the job, and any likelihood of me achieving this mythical upward mobility is little to none.

I don't blame you, Kevin, for the way I was treated originally, but I do blame you for the way I continue to be treated. People watch fake-ass hoaxers like you on the internet, someone who obviously has a screw or two loose, and they assume that anyone who claims to have seen a Bigfoot, like myself, is batshit crazy. Just because you're batshit crazy doesn't mean I'm batshit crazy, but I cannot convince others of this.

It's safe to say that my experience with Bigfoot has ruined my life, and I certainly wish that you would stop your shenanigans, because you make the case for people like me a lot worse.

I hate you,

Rex in Maine

P.S.- This won't be the last you hear of me.

The End

8

Riding That Dame High On Cocaine

*From a letter dated January 5, 2021

Dear Kevin,

First of all, I want to commend you for the work you do in a field few others would touch due to the sure fired guarantee that they will be ridiculed, mocked and discredited. You are a shining beacon in a world gone dark of real heroes. I commend you.

I thank God for you, because I now have a safe place I can come to with my story. For years, the raw emotions inside me, raw emotions brought about by an experience I had years ago that have never lessened in rawness, because until now, I've never been able to tell my tale.

You see, Kevin, I am an educated professional. I have a master's degree in business, and I am very successful. I earn more than a quarter of a million dollars a year as a private financial advisor. I work exclusively with high net worth individuals, and as such, I only have to have a couple of dozen clients to make the money that I do. I do not work with anyone who is not willing to bring me at least two millions dollars.

I state all this not to brag, or to sound like the arrogant prick that many people in my line of work are, but to make it clear to you why I have never come forward with my story until now. I would no doubt be written off as insane, and who, especially among high net worth individuals is going to invest their life savings with a man who is insane? I know I wouldn't.

So here's the story.

I haven't always been an upstanding member of my small community. Small community here, being the key phrase, as you know how people talk so much in small towns. And once branded bad, you stay bad.

Sure, I was always good at covering my tracks, and one of the ways I did so was by being bad, as it were, *outside* of my community, and this is where my profession came into play so well.

You see, I wasn't always a private financial planner. I used to work for a major brokerage firm, and I won't name which one, but I've followed your videos long enough to know that you used to do the same thing, and though you've never mentioned the large firm you used to work for, I have reason to believe it was the same one I worked for. The cultures sound too similar for the firms to be different.

Anyway, once per quarter, our firm would hold a regional meeting. These were basically 'rah rah' sessions where our region's top producers would sit on a podium and tell all of us underlings how great they were and why they were so great. You used to work in the business, so I know that you know how it all went. They would make it sound like they were Billy Badass, and like they basically told their clients to invest all their money with them, the way they told them to invest it, or else. And the clients would tremble in fear and not just open their checkbooks but run out to the banks and finance companies after leaving the office to borrow more money to invest with these Billy Badass brokers.

Of course, Billy Badass always left a hole in their stories. A big one. The part about how their mothers were the sweet little old ladies who everyone loved in the H.R. department down at the factory that employed ninety five percent of the town's working populations. And how that dear, little old lady (mom) handed each new retiree her son's business card and said, "Okay, now that you're retiring, you need to go see Jasper here, and make sure to do a 401k rollover. And you can't wait on this. Here, as a matter of fact, I'm gonna call and schedule your appointment."

They leave out the part of how the retirees just couldn't believe that the little old lady in the H.R. department that they loved so much already was actually calling Jasper for them and setting up their appointment, and why, how good it felt and how easy it was just to walk into Jasper's office on their way home that day, their last day of their thirty five years long career at the plant and sign papers to allow Jasper (such a fine, outstanding young man any mother would be proud of, though they'd never learn that the little old lady back at H.R. actually was Jasper's mother- that whole conflict of interest thing), to transfer all six hundred and fifty thousand of their 401k dollars into an IRA at Jasper's firm.

Anyway, after a while, and after I'd garnered enough of a book of business on my own (like you, I'm a self made man- I had no contacts in the real world), I said fuck 'em all and went independant.

However, it was during the last regional meeting I attended while still with the big brokerage firm that I had my experience with a creature that is not supposed to exist. An experience that would reshape the rest of my life, as I have not, and I repeat, I have NOT ventured into the woods since.

And this was back in 1986!

Okay, so I've aged myself, but that's okay, because you've got to understand the time when this happened, because a lot of what was going on had everything to do with the time. And I know you're probably too young to remember some of the most unflattering parts of the era.

So back in the mid 1980's, while you were probably watching a shitty movie remake of Flash Gordon (the old t.v. show I watched as a youth was way better) and Footloose, and listening to Culture Club and Cindy Lauper, those of us who were of age, and who worked in professional circles, were doing mountains of cocaine and throwing our car keys into salad bowls or hats at parties and then pulling out someone else's keys and then going home and having sex with whomever owned the keys we pulled from the hat or salad bowl.

Yes, I hate to admit that this is how I spent much of my late twenties and early thirties, but alas, it is. The past is the past, and I cannot change it. And besides, I don't think I'd want to, anyway. Some of my associates had some pretty hot wives.

Okay, so we were at a place you might actually know. Smith Mountain Lake, in the southern portion of Virginia (yes, I live in Virginia, too). We were partying balls that night after having our awards dinner, where we saw the Jaspers of the firm given huge accolades for having done more than a million dollars in gross production (though they should have given the award to their mothers, whom they never even mentioned). After our first round of cocaine, someone started passing the salad bowl. I dropped my keys in, and realizing I was the last in line, I went ahead and pulled out a pair as well.

I'll admit, I cheated. Our regional leader's wife was smoking hot. She was the typical trophy wife these guys would marry. And while she'd been walking around during dinner just hours earlier, she'd left her keychain conveniently hanging out of the side of her purse. To this day I remember it. It looked like Prince's white guitar that he made famous in the movie Purple Rain. Oh, how I miss the eighties.

Anyway, having had the hots for this woman since I'd first seen her, about two years earlier, I pulled her keys from the hat, and in pretty short order, she and I were walking through the woods surrounding the lake, hand in hand, looking for a secluded area.

Most of the other folks at the party were simply going to each other's cabins, but for some reason, this woman, Judy was her name, wanted to do it outside. Looking back on it, I think it is because she loved not letting her husband know who she'd had sex with during those escapades. Of all the couples who were honest with each other during those times, I never remember any of them breaking up when we all grew up, which was quickened by the advent of the AIDS virus. But among those who were secretive, I would say they all got divorced by the 1990's. I think Judy wanted to be able to hold secrets over her husband's head in order to make him both paranoid and jealous.

Anyway, I'm happy to report two things. Judy and I got it on hot and heavy, and secondly, I didn't catch anything that I couldn't wash off. Again, when I look back on how I lived all those years ago, it amazes me that I'm still here. Thank God for good luck and three different rehabs, the third of which took. Twenty three years clean and sober now, by the grace of God and a secret society I'm not allowed to mention in the press, radio or film (wink, wink).

Anyway, I'll be discreet in saving you the details of mine and Judy's quick escapade, but what I won't spare you is any detail in regard to the hideous creature we encountered on our way back to the party cabin.

Kevin, I know that you like to think of these creatures as being kind and benevolent. I can tell you they are not. Not that the beast that Judy and I encountered harmed a single hair on our head, because it didn't, but because of the look of death it wore on its face and the howl from hell that it emitted.

Imagine, there you are, walking down a moonlit path in the forest, having had just made love to the most beautiful woman you've ever known personally, actually fantasizing about ways to break her and her husband up (I actually was not married at the time), so that you could spend happily ever after with her (and of course, removing the idea from your head that she would want to be shared with others at social get togethers), when a beast standing nearly eight feet tall and weighing nearly eight hundred pounds just jumps out onto the trail in front of you. Well, that's exactly what happened to us.

"Oh, shit!" Judy yelled. "I knew we were snorting some bad blow!" Somehow, at the regional meeting before this one, we'd gotten ahold of some bad shit. It had been laced with something, and a couple of the brokers and their wives ended up the E.R. It turned out to be a good thing, actually, because while there, they all tested positive for Hepatitis C, and one was found to be carrying the AIDS virus. So had we never gotten that bad blow, those who were sick, but who did not know it, might not have found out until it was too late. And by the way, the cheap ass broker who brought the bad blow was asked to leave the firm the following week and he went into private practice, which he'd planned on doing, anyway. It didn't help him that his wife was a heifer and no one ever wanted to end up with her keys at a party.

Anway, I assured Judy that we were not on a bad trip (even though we weren't doing acid, but you know what I mean). I assured her the thing in front of us was real, very real, and that we were probably going to die.

The thing started walking toward us, slowly, sniffing as it did, trying to figure out what we were, though I have every reason to believe that it already knew. Sure, it may have never been seen by humans before, but I'm sure it had seen plenty of humans in its past.

The damn thing got only feet away from us, looking at us like a midnight snack, working its sniffer like there was no tomorrow. To this day, I have no idea how I came up with the idea, I guess it just came to me, but I did it, and it worked.

What am I talking about?

Cocaine!

I had a vile of cocaine in my pocket. I reached into my pocket with my left hand to pull it out and took up Judy's left hand with my right. Thank the God of your choosing, as you would say, that she had long, luxurious nails.

"What are you doing?" she asked. She was terrified of what was in front of us and of what I was doing, and she was also frozen stiff due to her terror, and I told her not to worry about it and to keep her mouth shut. Fortunately for both of us, she did.

I spread a line of coke out on Judy's pinky nail and I held her hand up toward the face of the monstrous beast that was now no less than an arm's length away from us. As I'd hoped would be the case, the creature sniffed the blow off of Judy's finger. It took a couple of steps back, sniffing violently as it did, and then came to a sudden stop.

I could tell from experience that the buzz had just kicked in full bore. I'm sure the creature had a pretty healthy, drug and alcohol free diet, which meant it had no tolerance to man made drugs. This thing was all jacked up on cocaine, and it started shaking, I mean its whole body, and it summarily let out a scream more terrifying than the scream it had emitted only a minute before.

I literally pissed my pants when the beast let out that second scream and Judy actually collapsed. And it was just then, when I thought the creature was going to rip us both limb from limb, that the creature began itching like crazy. I know that if you take too many prescription pills you'll itch like that (did I mention three rehabs? I think I did), so I just assumed the creature was having some sort of allergic reaction to the blow. Whatever the case was, it took off into the forest, disappearing as quickly and mysteriously as it had appeared. I heard it running for all it was worth, until I couldn't hear it running anymore, and then I heard a super loud splash. I guess it jumped into the lake, hoping the water would cure it of its itch. Sadly, it had no idea that the only true remedy for a bad trip and a hangover is time.

I bent over Judy and coaxed her to consciousness by slapping her, lightly and painlessly, on the cheek. When she came to, she had absolutely no recollection of what had just happened. Actually, she had no recollection of us having had sex, and she told me that I was gross and how in God had she pulled my keys, and for me to take her back to the party shack.

Fantasy over.

But the good news is, Judy never remembered our encounter with Bigfoot Sasquatch. At least not that she ever spoke of, and I honestly believe that she does not remember. This is good, because she was never able to pull me into having to talk about what had happened, which would surely have discredited me and I'm sure it would have ruined my life.

Jesus Christ, Kevin, it has been so many years that I've held this story inside of me, and I have wanted so badly to share it with someone, and finally, Thank God for you, because you are that someone.

I know that assholes who have no life and who live in their mother's basement give you ever loving hell in the comment section of your YouTube channel due to the videos you make. But listen, they are going to do that no matter what type of videos you make. Those people are just miserable and hate their lives. You could go back to making those boring ass videos about green beans and corn and you'll still have them. So please, please, pretty please, whatever you do, do NOT stop making your Bigfoot Sasquatch videos. I don't know if this goes as far as some sort of Government coverup, but I do know that these creatures are out here, and the masses need to be informed. So please, keep being that shining beckon in the dark for those of us who you are so bravely leading to your light.


Sincerely yours,


P.T.

Somewhere in Southwestern Virginia


The End

Oh Well, Anyway

Kevin,

First of all, I want to let you know that I love your YouTube channel "Homesteading Off The Grid." I hated it when your giggly wife, Dearly, stopped making videos with you, but I can understand the fear and concern she had with all things Bigfoot Sasquatch. I'm glad she started her own channel, "Life With Dearly," and as with your channel, I never miss a single one of her videos. She is such a sweet little lady. I'm a retired RN from a nursing home and I used to work with a Filipina lady who looked almost identical to Dearly. We're still friends. She's a lot younger than me and she still works. I showed her one of Dearly's videos and told her I thought they two of them looked alike and she just laughed, and when she did, she kind of sounded like Dearly, too.

Oh, well.

Anyway, I wanted to let you know that I love your approach to Bigfoot Sasquatch. The way you don't claim that him, her, it or they are definitely real or that him, her, it or they definitely are not real. You keep an open minded approach that I believe would make the world a better place if more people could do the same about more topics. Like you, I absolutely hate politics, and I'm glad that you never discuss them on your channel. I have seen that issue divide the best of friends and the closest of family members, but I guess that's the underlying purpose of the two party system, anyway.

Oh, well.

No room for gray. It's got to be either black or white, and you're either for 'em or you're again' 'em, or you're not welcome in their home, by God. At least that seems to be the belief system of so many single minded assholes who are absorbed with the issues. Look at me. Just discussing the idea of politics gets me worked up.

Oh, well.

Anyway, here's why I'm writing, and thank you for setting up a P.O. box. I hope you got my Christmas card. You never said. But I saw the fistfuls of cards you were getting in a couple of your videos you made around the holidays and I understand.

Oh, well.

Anyway, I have never seen Bigfoot Sasquatch. However, my grandfather, back when he was alive- and this was a long time ago, as he died when I was still in grade school, and I was born in 1950, so do the math- used to always tell us a story about having seen something in the forests of Pennsylvania back when he was a kid that very much sounded like a Bigfoot Sasquatch to me.

Now, my grandfather claims to have had his experience when he was about thirteen years old, so that would have had to have been just before the turn of the last century. Probably in the 1890's. Wow! It blows my mind to even think of a time back that far.

Oh, well.

Anyway, my grandfather used to love to fish for these tiny little native brook trout. Small fish that were not stocked by the hatcheries. They existed in just about every little creek or stream that flowed through most mountains in Appalachiastan. We grew up in the rust belt portion of Pennsylvania, just south of Pittsburgh and not far from the West Virginia border.

My grandfather had always been a loner. I guess going back to birth. So it comes as no surprise that on the day of his experience, he was alone.

It's a pretty simple story, really. Grandaddy said he was catching so many fish on this particular day that he was leaving them all strung in groups on lengths of fishing line, scattered on the bank of the stream he was fishing that day. His plan was to collect each string filled with small trout on his way back downstream. Grandaddy always said that one of his few regrets in life is having kept every single fish he ever caught and taking it home to eat. He said that times were tough back then, and they needed the food, and not a single critter he ever killed went uneaten, but it broke his heart that by the time he was an old man, many of the streams that used to be filled with "tubs of fish" as he always put it, when he'd been younger, "didn't have a blame fish in 'em," as he also put it.

Oh, well.

Anyway, he had caught nearly a hundred fish on that particular day, and as he was heading back down stream, collecting them all, he came around a sharp bend in the river, and just as he popped around the bend, something huge, as in eight feet tall and eight hundred pounds, stood up downstream. It had been crouched down. Grandaddy said when it stood up that it was holding one of his strings filled with small trout.

Grandaddy said the strangest part of it all was that he was never scared. He never felt threatened or as if he was in harm's way. He said he actually felt a sense of peace.

Grandaddy said that big 'ol thing that took his fish merely walked across the stream, heading away from Grandaddy, and disappeared into the woods.

No one, for Grandaddy's entire life, ever doubted Grandaddy's story. Sure, there were folks who would say that it was probably a bear, but no one ever called Grandaddy a liar. Grandaddy would go on to work in the steel mills until he retired, and his story would never change.

Anyway, I've been reading your "Bigfoot Sasquatch Files" books and when I read the story of you and your old college roomate going fishing and having that big 'ol brown trout stolen from you by a bear, who in turn had it stolen from him by a Bigfoot Sasquatch, I just felt like I had to share my Grandaddy's story with you. I hope you liked it, and you can share it with other people if you want. Just don't tell them my name, because I see how rude people are to you on your YouTube channel, just for making silly videos. I don't want any part of that.

Oh, well.

Anyway, have a great day and give my best to your beautiful family!

Yours Truly,


R.G.

Somerset, Pennsylvania


The End

There's Only Room In This World For One Bigfoot Sasquatch

*Author's explanation: One of the biggest time consuming tasks for social media content creators, which is also one of the least liked activities for social content creators, is 'policing your page or site or channel, etc.' This basically involves going through the comment section a couple times a day and banning people who post inappropriate comments. Many people claim this is a violation of 'free speech' but it is anything but. You see, most viewers of YouTube channels, in time, actually come to care for the content creator, albeit, from afar (unless they have issues with boundaries and end up becoming stalkers, which was discussed at the beginning of this book). And when they see their favorite YouTuber constant getting bashed and berated in the comment section, they will actually stop coming around, because they do not like it. And, people commenting in our YouTube channel's comment section, asking me such questions as "how much did it cost to mail your mail order bride to the U.S.?" and "was your wife even eighteen when you started fucking her?" which, believe it or not, are comments we receive daily, all these years into our social media careers, are hardly representations of free speech. It is one thing to have the right to state your comments, opinions or beliefs in regard to any situation or topic, but referring the woman that I love as a mail order bride, or a whore (we get that one a lot), or to me as a pedophile, is not free speech. That's being an asshole, and those assholes are summarily banned.

I do an excellent job of policing my channel's comment section, which is great for our supportive viewers, but what I can tell you is that starting your day, each and every day, before the sun comes up, blocking all the assholes who hit your hard during the night while you slept is not an enjoyable experience. In time, I do believe it will lead me out of being a YouTuber. Imagine if you will, every morning for the past five years, waking up, having coffee, and then reading dozens of comments telling you how much you suck, how you are a liar, a scammer, etc. (and don't forget, a pedophile), and that the woman you love more than life is an opportunistic whore.

Anyway, there is one particular type of troll that has stood out over the course of the past two years that we've been doing the Bigfoot Sasquatch stuff on our YouTube channel 'Homesteading Off The Grid." And it's not the "you're a chime-o and your wife's a whore," type of troll. And it's not even the smartest guy in the room type troll who comes on and claims there is no such thing as Bigfoot sasquatch and then states that all our viewers are a bunch of ignorant, inbred hillbillies (yes, this is one of our most common forms of trolls). It's the trolls who absolutely believe in Bigfoot Sasquatch, claim to have had an experiences with him, her, it or they, yet for some reason, think that no one else can have a Bigfoot Sasquatch living in the woods behind their home, because, by God, they're the only ones allowed to have a Bigfoot Sasquatch living in the woods behind their home. Ironically, and not by much of a surprise, many of these vertically challenged individuals who live under bridges have small, dickless YouTube channels and they (surprise, surprise) make videos about Bigfoot Sasquatch, and they usually have all of fifteen or twenty subscribers and in truth, they're trying to drive my viewers to their channels. It amazes me how some people simply never learn two things. 1- the golden rule, and 2- you draw more flies with honey than vinegar.

At any rate, here are a few recent examples of people who I've recently prayed for (God, please bring this vertically challenged individual who lives under a bridge the same health, wealth and prosperity you have so blessed my family and me with), and then summarily banned!

~ This guy is a liar. I can't believe he has so many subscribers. I know Bigfoot is real, because I've seen him, but this guy hasn't. He's doing this for money, because he gets money from YouTube, and all you idiots are falling for it. I'm out. Come watch my channel. Where shit is real.

~ I live in Washington State, and I have had first hand encounters with Sasquatch. Everyone knows he lives in the Pacific Northwest. Where is this guy even at? Somewhere in the south? He talks like a hick. I know he's lying. There are no Sasquatches in the south. It's too fucking hot for them.

~ I know this guy is a liar and a fake, but I know Bigfoot is real. We have one in our woods. But we live in Oregon, where Bigfoot does, too. Who has ever heard of Bigfoot living in the south? I hope this guy loses his YouTube channel. His videos are a complete waste of bandwidth.

~ Anything for attention. I know Bigfoot is real. I saw him while hiking in the Rocky's many years ago. I have always kept it to myself, because I don't want the attention. But you can tell this guy is lying. There are too many tells. He just wants attention. All you people who are buying this need to stop giving it to him. It's the only way he'll ever go away. By the way, I never go back to Colorado, because I never want to see Bigfoot again.

~ You can tell these videos are staged. Sure, bigfoot is real, but this guy is fake. If you really want to see a channel that has real bigfoots in it, come to my channel. Please subscribe to it and tell all of your friends to do the same. This guy is a flim flam man.

~ When I was a small child, hiking through the woods with my daddy, I saw a bigfoot. My daddy told me never to tell anyone, because he said it lived in the woods behind our house. I never saw it again, but I know it's back there, all these years later. That's how I know this guy is fake. Yes, bigfoot is real, but he lives in the woods behind my house, and I live in Arkansas. This man claims to be in Virginia, and that's probably a lie, too, but let's give him the benefit of the doubt and say he's up there in Virginia, well then, like I said, he's a liar, because Bigfoot's down here in Arkansas.

~ My husband and I used to be the most outdoorsy couple you'd ever meet. Our love story is one that goes back to childhood. We actually met at 4-H camp, which shows how long we've both been together and outdoorsy. We're in our late forties now, though we don't look like it, because though we're not outdoorsy anymore, for reasons you'll soon understand, we still work out all the time, but in the safe confines of a gym.

Anyway, while on a hiking trip in Idaho, just outside of Coeur D'alene, back at the turn of the current century, we saw something on the trail ahead of us, coming right at us, that was, without a doubt, a Bigfoot Sasquatch. At first, we thought that once it saw us, it would simply turn and run the other way, but that's not what happened.

As we stood there, too afraid to move, we saw that the thing had clearly spotted us. Then, it threw its nose up in the air and started sniffing around. Then, it came running toward us!

"Oh, shit!" I screamed. "I'm on my period!" And I was, and my husband knew I was, because he wanted to start that day with a romp in the sack, but we didn't because of it.

Anyway, I knew that if Bigfoot caught us, he was going to kill my husband and rape me. We have never run as fast as we did that day before or since that day, and we both do 5K charity runs on a regular basis, so that tells you something. We're good runners, and we love giving.

Anyway, we made it safely to our car, a hybrid I'd like to point out, back before hybrids were cool, and though we hated to do it, we decided to become gerbils on treadmills rather than free range spirits in the wild. Though we still run our 5k's, we only run them in the cities, because we love running and we're so giving, and because everyone knows Bigfoot isn't in the cities.

Which brings me to my main point!

Everyone knows there's no bigfoot in the woods behind this guy's house. Virginia? Seriously? Fat rednecks and hillbilly transplants from nearby Appalachia? Sure! Bigfoot? No way. This guy is a liar, and everyone knows it. Does he even run?

The End

(I wish it were, but there'll be more like this tomorrow morning when I wake up.)

11

Bigfoot Sasquatch Beat Him Into Serenity

*From a letter dated 01-13-2021

Dear Kevin,

I have been an avid follower of your YouTube channel "Homesteading Off The Grid" since before you went big. I remember I was one of your first one hundred subscribers. I was happy for you and your family when you went viral with the crayon video, which allowed you to quit your 'job you hated that made you miserable' down at the post office.

Now, with that said, I was a little hesitant about all your Bigfoot Sasquatch videos once they started, but not because I didn't believe- trust me, I'm a believer- or because I thought you were making fun of those of us who do believe, because I knew you were not. You have a very dry, witty sense of humor that can come across as something it's not to both the less intelligent who simply don't get it, as well as the intellectual elitists who take themselves too seriously to know humor when it presents itself- the smartest guys in the room, as you call them on your YouTube channel. However, I pride myself in being a middler, as Ben Franklin called us, and I get the humor quick and fast, and I am very appreciative of it, especially in this overly serious, overly politicized and overly polarized world.

Why did your Bigfoot Sasquatch videos bother me so much then, you might ask?

Because they simply hit too close to home.

Yes, Kevin, and anyone you care to share this story with (I do give you permission to do so, but please edit my writing first so I don't look uneducated ((*Author's/editor's/Crazy Lake's note- DONE!))), I do have quite the Bigfoot Sasquatch story to tell.

I'm well into retirement now, and I have a wife of more than thirty years, and we raised two kids who I hope turn out okay. So far so good, but they are in their twenties, and they don't seem to know how to hold a conversation that isn't digital. However, I am very proud of the fact that neither of them are violent. They are very peaceful.

And this brings me to my story.

When I was a kid, growing up in Appalachia, like you did, (but a different part of Appalachiastan, not West "By God" Virginia), I was as much a product of hillbilly culture as I'm sure you were and still are, though I'm sure, like me, you fight it. I was quick to anger, I was defensive, and I was insecure as all get out, as we'd say back there back then (I got out, too, and as you can tell by my return address, I now live in Ohio), and would rather punch it out than talk it out, whatever the it was.

I wasn't a big guy, but I was mean as a rattlesnake. For a guy to be named Stacey, like me, you can imagine the bullying one would procure. In traditional hillbilly fashion, anytime anyone picked on me because of my name, calling me a girl and all, I'd light into them like a bolt of lighting. Being as my persecutors were hillbillies as well, they never learned their lesson, nor quit just because of a good old fashioned hillbilly ass whoopin', and they'd come at me again the next day.

However, there was another reason I was always fighting. I had an older brother, who died many years ago now due to health complications associated with a lifetime of illnesses and physical deformities, who all the other kids liked to pick on as well. We all know the saying, "kids can be so cruel." As you know, Kevin, make those kids hillbilly kids in Appalachia and it gets even worse.

My parents, from the time I could remember, put me in charge of my brother's wellbeing when we were out of their sight. While we were out playing, or in the woods, and especially at school. I didn't mind, at first, as it made me feel important- responsible- but in time, this duty became too much for a young child to bear. Not only did I have to defend myself from my own bullies, those mean hillbilly kids who saw fit to make fun of my name, but I also had to defend my brother from all the little assholes who chose to pick on him for having been born differently than they were. And to add insult to injury, if I didn't do it, or if I simply hadn't been with my brother during a time when he'd been bullied, my parents would light my ass up with the buckle end of a belt when I got home.

Anyway, fast forward to our teen years. You can imagine throwing the hormones of puberty into this mix, and I was a hot mess. I was even more angry than usual, fighting and getting into trouble more often, and I remember feeling like I wanted to either run away or die. The only good part of the story during those days is that the beatings at home stopped, because when I was fifteen, I took the belt away from my step father (mom's third husband), and beat holy hell out of him with it. No one in that household ever touched me again.

Though I might be proud of having dealt out an asswhoopin' as a fifteen year old kid to an abusive adult who deserved it, a year after that, I dealt out an asswhoopin' to someone who didn't deserve it.

My brother.

A bunch of us had gone camping up at this old abandoned cabin that used to be occupied by moonshiners back in the day. As always, I had to take my brother with me. My friends were used to this by now, but you see, we had something with us, rather, we'd found something under the old floor boards of that old cabin, that we weren't used to.

Moonshine!

Sure, we'd sneaked the occasional Stroh's beer (and I know you know what that is, since you're a hillbilly, too), from our step-fathers, but we'd never had liquor, especially white lightning. Suffice to say, we got pretty well lit up pretty quick.

For some reason, my brother started talking about Bigfoot. He claimed that during many of the times he slipped away, without anyone knowing exactly where he was, he was up in those very woods where we were camping, hanging out with Bigfoot.

Well, our two other friends who were with us started making fun of my brother for this, and before they even knew what day of the week it was I'd lit into them and whooped 'em both and told 'em to head on off the hill before I put 'em in a grave. They didn't need to be told twice.

I watched those two boys leave, and then I turned around and looked at my brother. I told him I was sick and tired of fighting his fights for him and that if he wasn't able to fight for himself, he needed to stop being such a dipshit. I remember to this day what happened next. He pointed behind me, smiled, and said "Bigfoot."

"You retarded mother fucker!" I said, and for the first and only time in our lives, I punched my brother square in the chin. The place I'd learn while in basic training in the Army (I was drafted during the Vietnam War), they called 'the button.' It's the place boxers aim for, because if you hit it square on, like I did with my brother, you knock your opponent out, and it doesn't even really take a whole lot of pressure.

Well, my brother hit the ground, and just a split second after he did, I heard a growl from behind me. I turned around, and there, only feet away, was…

…you guessed it…

…Bigfoot Sasquatch!

And let me tell ya, it wasn't one of those experiences you hear so much about, where the creature and I made eye contact, and I wet my pants, and the creature turned and ran away, and then I told people about it and it ruined my life, etc. etc. I mean, all that happened, except for the creature turning away part. Oh, it didn't turn away. No, sir!

It gave me one rightly deserved asswhoopin'!

But it was the strangest asswhoopin' I could have imagined.

It didn't really hurt!

You see, the creature didn't rip my head off with his brute strength. He (or she, or it, as you'd say on your YouTube channel) didn't slice and dice me (as we said about the bayonet in the infantry) with its super sharp claws. It simply picked me up and held me above its at least eight feet tall head, and then it threw me down to the ground. And then it did it again.

And again.

And again.

And again!

It was as if the creature was trying to punish me for what I'd done to my brother. But unlike my hillbilly parents and step-parents, it wasn't punishing me, while angry, trying to hurt me for what I'd done- a style of punishment I'd fortunately learn in my own adult years is never acceptable- but it was trying to discipline me out of caring- out of the desire to let me know I'd done wrong and my behavior was not acceptable.

After the beast threw me down for what would be the last time, and then turned and walked away, I felt an odd feeling come over me. It wasn't fear and it wasn't anger. For the first time in my life, I had a sense of serenity. The beast had actually beaten me into a sense of serenity! Other than watching my children enter the world, it is the closest thing to a spiritual experience I've ever had.

When I sat up, my brother was jumping up and down, clapping his hands, saying "Bigfoot! Bigfoot!" over and over.

I stood, dusted my britches off, and I walked up to my brother and I told him I was sorry. He just smiled and laughed and kept saying Bigfoot over and over, like I'd never hit him in the first place. I gave him a big hug and I never hurt him again.

And amazingly, I never hurt anyone else after that, either.

After that experience with this amazing creature that is not supposed to exist, I never had a temper problem. My fuse, which had always been so short, became so lengthy no one could ever burn it down to the detonator.

The following year was my senior year in high school. My teachers noticed the change in me, and upon the urging of our guidance counselor, I actually went to college (a small in state school, but hey, college was like a foreign nation to my family and all the other hillbillies around us), and I graduated, and I was able to leave Appalachiastan and lead what many would call an average, middle class American life, but a life, which as you know, is anything but average when you come from an Appalachian background.

Sadly, my brother passed away before I finished college. He'd outlived the life expectancy they'd given him at birth by many years, so we knew we were blessed to have him when we did and for much longer than we should have, but to this day, his passing is the second biggest heartache I've experienced, the first, of course, being the heartache associated with the time I whooped up on him up there in the woods.

Kevin, I commend you for doing the work that you're doing with your YouTube channel. You are bringing awareness to many people that there are things in this world that are not supposed to exist, but do. And I can't even tell you how much I related to so many of the stories in your completely awesome short story collection, "October Nights." I bought a print copy of the book on Amazon as soon as it came out, and admittedly, read the entire thing before the month of October even rolled around. But I didn't regret it, because having done so allowed me to sit and watch and listen as you read each story from the book each night of October on your YouTube channel. That was a great experience that I hope you do again next fall. I saw some reviews of your book on Amazon that were not flattering due to this fact. People actually giving you shitty reviews because you read the stories on YouTube. I guess they felt like they'd wasted their money buying the book, because they could have just listened to the stories on your YouTube channel, but I guess those people have no idea what it's like to grow up poor in

Appalachia, and not have the resources to buy a book (something that is simple for me now, thank God), and have no one care, because you don't belong to the right demographic that garners special interest votes come election day.

Sorry for that digression, as I know you despise politics, as do I, and I'm sure for much of the same reason. Our hillbilly roots.

Anway, I just wanted to send you this letter and share my Bigfoot Sasquatch experience with you and anyone else who would be interested in either hearing about it on your YouTube channel or reading about it in one of your upcoming "Bigfoot Sasquatch Files" volumes, frankly, which is where I'd like to see it, because I've read every one of them and anxiously anticipate the publication of each new volume. (*Author's/editor's/Crazy Lake's note- DONE!)

It's my hope and wish that God continues to bless you and your beautiful little family there on your beautiful little homestead in Virginia. It looks like the perfect place. The beauty of nearby Appalachiastan, without all the dysfunction of, not all, but so damn many of its people.

Your forever fan and YouTube viewer,


Stacey P.

Akron, Ohio


The End

*If you enjoyed this work, please consider reading more from author Kevin "Crazy" Lake, whose books are available in print or Kindle on Amazon.

Made in the USA
Monee, IL
26 February 2021